Slothy Claus

A Christmas Story

By Jodie Shepherd

Illustrated by MacKenzie Haley

An Imprint of Thomas Nelson

Slothy Claus

© 2021 Thomas Nelson

Tommy Nelson, PO Box 141000, Nashville, TN 37214

Published in Nashville, Tennessee, by Tommy Nelson. Tommy Nelson is an imprint of Thomas Nelson. Thomas Nelson is a registered trademark of HarperCollins Christian Publishing, Inc.

Tommy Nelson titles may be purchased in bulk for educational, business, fund-raising, or sales promotional use. For information, please email SpecialMarkets@ThomasNelson.com.

ISBN 978-1-4002-2359-6 (eBook)
ISBN 978-1-4002-2358-9 (HC)

Library of Congress Cataloging-in-Publication Data

Names: Shepherd, Jodie, author. | Haley, MacKenzie, illustrator. | Moore, Clement Clarke, 1779-1863. Night before Christmas.
Title: Slothy Claus : a Christmas story / by Jodie Shepherd ; illustrated by MacKenzie Haley.
Description: Nashville, Tennessee : Thomas Nelson, [2021] | Audience: Ages 4-8. | Summary: Slothy Claus slowly loads his sleigh, taking breaks for naps and snacks, and finally makes his deliveries long after the forest animals have discovered that the blessings of Christmas can come without presents. Told in the rhythm of Clement Moore's "Night before Christmas."
Identifiers: LCCN 2020054855 (print) | LCCN 2020054856 (ebook) | ISBN 9781400223589 (hardcover) | ISBN 9781400223596 (epub)
Subjects: CYAC: Stories in rhyme. | Christmas--Fiction. | Sloths--Fiction. | Forest animals--Fiction. | Humorous stories.
Classification: LCC PZ8.3.S551 Slo 2021 (print) | LCC PZ8.3.S551 (ebook) | DDC [E]--dc23
LC record available at https://lccn.loc.gov/2020054855
LC ebook record available at https://lccn.loc.gov/2020054856

Written by Jodie Shepherd
Illustrated by MacKenzie Haley

Printed in Malaysia

21 22 23 24 25 IMG 6 5 4 3 2 1

Mfr: IMG / Rawang, Malaysia / September 2021 / PO #9589891

'Twas the night before Christmas,
and everyone knew
they'd soon get a visit from,
well, **you-know-who.**

With his **long**, furry arms
and his STRONG

three-toed paws

and his sweet
and slow smile,

it was ol'
Slothy Claus!

So creatures hung stockings and made their trees **pretty,**

all through the forests,
in country and city.

They set out
slothy treats,
like a mango
or cherry,

as thanks for a holiday sure to be merry.

MEANWHILE . . .

Slothy *slooooooooooooooc*

ooooowly ...

. . . but surely was
packing the sled
while wishing he still

was ASLEEP in his bed.

He piled up
the boxes,
at least two
or three.

Then he took
a short nap.

He was
TIRED
as could be.

MEANWHILE . . .

The next morning the sun rose all **shiny** and bright.

And what **do** you think had arrive**d** in the night?

NOTHING!

That's what! 'Cause **no one** had come.

There weren't
any games,
not a book,
not a drum.

MEANWHILE . . .

Slothy Claus *slooowly* piled up some more boxes.

There were gifts for bear families, for rabbits and foxes.

TAKE IT EASY

Christmas sleighs me

To:
From:

sloth life

But the work was so hard.
So he stopped for a bite.

Not a thing to unwrap,
and no sweets to enjoy.

How could
Christmas
have passed
without even
one toy?

The stockings
were empty;

the floor,
it was **bare**

'cause ol' **Slothy Claus**
just hadn't
been there.

At first the strange Christmas
had made them all sad.

But then they took stock of the things that they had.
They had love. They had hope.
They had kindness and grace.
They had joy and good fortune all over the place!

And they had one another! What more could they need?
So life in the forest was happy indeed.

Who cared if ol' Slothy was far or was near—
the blessings of Christmas came all through the year.

THEN ONE DAY . . .

The weather was hot, and the flowers were blooming,
and nobody noticed the sled that was zooming.

Well, maybe not zooming,
but it *was* coming near.

It was July, and finally,

Slothy was here!

It was Christmas AT LAST,
although Christmas had passed.

But with or without a cold wintry blast,
Christmas had lived in their hearts all along.
So after he joined in some dancing and song . . .

Slothy exclaimed as his sled rose in flight,

"Merry Christmas to all,
and to all a good night!"

For Lisa, Kathie & Ryan, and Mom, Dad & Willow —M.L. and J.V.

To Tonia and Brian Simpson, for believing their eldest daughter about who she was —D.S.

Text copyright © 2020 by Maddox Lyons and Jessica Verdi
Illustrations copyright © 2020 by Dana Simpson
Published by Roaring Brook Press
Roaring Brook Press is a division of Holtzbrinck Publishing Holdings Limited Partnership
120 Broadway, New York, NY 10271
mackids.com

Library of Congress Control Number: 2019948769
ISBN: 978-0-374-31068-4

Our books may be purchased in bulk for promotional, educational, or business use. Please contact your local bookseller or the Macmillan Corporate and Premium Sales Department at (800) 221-7945 ext. 5442 or by email at MacmillanSpecialMarkets@macmillan.com.

First edition, 2020
Book design by Aram Kim
Printed in China by Toppan Leefung Printings Ltd., Dongguan City, Guangdong Province

10 9 8 7 6 5 4 3 2 1